Twinkle, Twinkle, Sparkly Star

by Katharine Holabird · illustrated by Sarah Warburton

Ready-to-Read

Simon Spotlight
New York London Toronto Sydney New Delhi

SIMON SPOTLIGHT

An imprint of Simon & Schuster Children's Publishing Division

1230 Avenue of the Americas, New York, New York 10020

This Simon Spotlight edition December 2020

Text copyright © 2020 by Katharine Holabird

Illustrations copyright © 2020 by Sarah Warburton

Illustrations by Cherie Zamazing

SIMON SPOTLIGHT, READY-TO-READ, and colophon are registered trademarks of Simon & Schuster, Inc.

For information about special discounts for bulk purchases, please contact Simon & Schuster Special Sales at 1-866-506-1949 or business@simonandschuster.com.

Manufactured in the United States of America 1020 LAK

10 9 8 7 6 5 4 3 2 1

Library of Congress Cataloging-in-Publication Data

Names: Holabird, Katharine, author. | Warburton, Sarah, illustrator. Title: Twinkle, twinkle, sparkly star / Katharine Holabird ; illustrated by Sarah Warburton. Description: Simon Spotlight edition. | New York : Simon Spotlight, 2020. | Series: Twinkle | Audience: Ages 5-7. | Audience: Grades K-1. | Summary: Twinkle practices and practices to be perfect in the school play, but her friends remind her she does not need to be perfect to shine like a star. Identifiers: LCCN 2020021356 | ISBN 9781534486232 (paperback) | ISBN 9781534486249 (hardcover) | ISBN 9781534486256 (eBook) Subjects: CYAC: Fairies—Fiction. | Theater—Fiction. | Friendship—Fiction. Classification: LCC PZ7.H689 Twnh 2020 | DDC [E]—dc23 LC record available at https://lccn.loc.gov/2020021356

Twinkle's wings glowed brightly.
"Did you hear the big news, Lulu?"
she asked.
"We are putting on a show
at school.
And we will all have parts in it!"

"How fun!" said Lulu.
"I hope I get to be the star!"
"I hope I get to sing," said Pippa.
"I hope I get to dance and sparkle!"
said Twinkle.
"Don't you want to be the star?"
asked Lulu.

"I am too shy," said Twinkle.
"I will dance and sparkle
around you on the stage."
"And then everyone will clap
and give us lovely flowers!"
said Pippa.
"Don't forget," said Twinkle.
"If you are the star,
you have to practice a lot."
"I can do that," said Lulu.

"Calling all fairies!"
said Miss Flutterbee.
"Today we will try out
for the school show.
Please do your best and also have fun.
I want to see everyone sparkle
onstage."

Everyone clapped at the end.
Twinkle stood in the middle
of the stage with Pippa and Lulu.
"Everyone tries their best,"
she whispered to them.
"But sometimes even a star
needs a little help."
Everyone cheered.
And all the fairies
glowed as bright as stars.

"You can do it, Twinks!" said Lulu.
With her friends next to her,
Twinkle smiled.
She sang and danced
and sparkled.

Then Pippa took Twinkle's hand.
They held hands and sang together.

Lulu took Twinkle's other hand.
The three fairies danced together.

She was the star!
Everyone was looking at her!
Twinkle felt nervous and shy.

Twinkle did not move.
All the fairies began
to sing and dance.
But not Twinkle.

Everyone stood in their places.
The curtain went up.
Bright lights were on the stage.
The music started.
And . . .

Finally, it was the day of the show.
"Are you ready to sparkle?"
asked Pippa.
"You are the star!" said Lulu.
"Places, everyone!"
called Miss Flutterbee.

Then all the little fairies
helped Twinkle.
Twinkle had so much fun dancing
with her friends,
her wings began to glow and sparkle.
She could remember all the steps!
She was not shy!

"Don't worry, Twinks," said Lulu
the next day at school.
"No one is perfect."
"We all make mistakes," said Pippa.
"Fairies just need to help each other."

Later, Twinkle practiced
singing and dancing
with her forest friends again.
Whenever Twinkle fell, or tripped,
or forgot her steps,
she got up and kept dancing.
She did not feel shy
with her forest friends.

The next day most of the little fairies
knew where to stand
and what to sing
and what steps to dance.
But Twinkle sometimes forgot.

The forest creatures came out
to help her.
They all sang and danced
with Twinkle.
"Thank you for helping me,"
said Twinkle.

Twinkle wanted to do her best.
She practiced singing and dancing
in her pod.
Then she practiced
singing and dancing
all over the Sparkle Tree Forest.

Twinkle was nervous.
She kept forgetting
where to stand
or when to sing
or what steps to dance.
"That is what practice is for!"
said Miss Flutterbee.
"We will try again tomorrow!"

After school the little fairies
started practicing for the show.
It was hard work!
Miss Flutterbee showed them
where to stand,
when to sing,
and what steps to dance.

"Twinkle!" said Lulu.
"You are the star!"
Pippa and Lulu skipped
around Twinkle.
But Twinkle was not sure
she was ready to be the star. . . .

All the fairies were reading
a list taped to the school door.
Twinkle looked at the list.
Lulu was a ladybug.
Pippa was a sunflower.
Twinkle looked for her name.
There it was at the top! Oh no!
"Twinkle . . . the star."

"Come on!" said Lulu.
"We want to see
who gets to be the star!" said Pippa.

the Fairy

The next morning Twinkle was
very sleepy.
She fluttered slowly to school
with Lulu and Pippa.

Twinkle went to bed early.
"Dancing fairies need a good rest,"
she said.
But that night Twinkle could not
sleep.
She wished she were not shy.
Then she could sing and dance
across the stage like Lulu.
Twinkle tossed and turned all night.

Miss Flutterbee smiled and clapped.
"All my little fairies were
wonderful!" she said.
"You will all help make this
the best show ever.
Go home and get some rest tonight.
Tomorrow we will practice our parts.
We will be very busy!"

Lulu was not shy at all.
She loved being onstage.
But Twinkle was shy.
She watched Lulu sing and dance
across the stage and back again.

"I can sing a song," said Lulu.

"I can dance and sparkle,"
said Twinkle.
She did a little dance.

"I can play music," said Pippa.

The fairies were excited.
Everyone lined up to
do their best for Miss Flutterbee.